The Peculiar Thing with the Pea

Kaye Umansky

With illustrations by
Claire Powell

For Alex – K.U.

*For Melissa, somewhere over the rainbow.
Love always – C.P.*

First published in 2020 in Great Britain by
Barrington Stoke Ltd
18 Walker Street, Edinburgh, EH3 7LP

www.barringtonstoke.co.uk

Text © 2020 Kaye Umansky
Illustrations © 2020 Claire Powell

A CIP catalogue record for this book is available
from the British Library upon request

ISBN: 978-1-78112-919-7

Printed by Hussar Books, Poland

Contents

Chapter 1

The Marriage Shock

"*Married?*" I said.

"Yes," said Mother.

"*Me* get married?"

"Yes," said Mother.

"But I'm eleven!"

We were sat round the breakfast table. Up to that moment, I had been in a happy mood. I had scoffed three bowls of cereal and was thinking about getting up a game of five-a-side football with the kitchen boys. Maybe throw a few stones in the moat. Relax with a comic.

"Yes, darling, I know you're only eleven. But getting married takes *years* to arrange. Doesn't it, Basil?"

My father looked up from the newspaper and said, "Mm?"

"I'm telling Pete that a royal wedding takes years to arrange."

"Mm," said my father. "Awful, awful."

"How come?" I asked.

"Well," said Mother, "first, we must find the right princess. Then both sets of parents have to meet. It takes for ever to set up a date for that, because kings and queens are busy people. I know *my* diary's full for the next three years, and Daddy's up to his ears, aren't you, Basil? Then all the papers have to be signed, the dowry agreed, bells rung, street parties, invitations, flowers, cake – it's endless."

She sounded quite excited at the thought. My father, not so much.

"I don't believe this," I said, wondering what a dowry was.

My father looked up from the sports page. "Pete," he said. "Fear not, son. Even if your mother finds a princess tomorrow, getting everything organised will take so long that you'll be old enough to collect your pension before you get hitched."

"So," said Mother, "we need to get started. I shall write to all the kings and queens I can think of who may have a daughter that Pete can marry."

"What if you don't find one?" I asked. Father's words had made me feel a bit calmer, but I still was not at all happy about the whole marriage idea – sooner, later, or even at all.

"If I don't get any answers from the kings and queens, then I'll have to put an advertisement in the *Royal Times*."

"Does it matter what *I* think about this?" I asked.

"Of course, darling! We'll organise a meeting with the chosen princess and see how you get on. We want you to be happy, Pete. We're not monsters. Have a lovely day, both of you."

Mother got up and told Creekie, the butler, to clear the table. She kissed my father and tried to kiss me too. I dodged, but she got me on the ear. Then she swept out.

"She didn't mention the pea thing," said Father.

"What pea thing?"

"The peculiar thing her family do with a pea."

"What peculiar thing?"

"Some silly test to find out if a princess is real. Your mother says that it will let her find out who the fakes are. Total nonsense, of course. I'll let her tell you about it." Father looked back at his paper. "I see they cancelled last Saturday's Knights versus Lords tournament. Mud stopped play."

We talked about tournaments, and I worried about getting married for a bit. But then I thought about it properly. How would my mother's letters even get anywhere? There is only one very old postman in the whole of the kingdom. His name is Mr Jones, and his donkey, who's just as old as him, is called Darby. Darby and Jones. If they went any slower, they'd go backwards. Mother's letters would take months to deliver. That's if they even arrived. Darby likes the odd paper snack, and royal letters are extra tasty. The whole marriage thing wasn't going to happen any time soon, if ever.

I went off to organise the kitchen boys versus gardener's boys match. I was on the gardening team. We won, 4–3. It was too cold to throw stones in the moat, so I went to my room and painted Sir Brett Boldfoot, my latest model knight. Knights are my hobby. I collect them, paint them, name them and set them out all over the floor, where they fight long, complicated knightly battles.

It was an OK day, actually. I forgot all about the marriage shock.

Until just over a week later.

Again, we were at the breakfast table. Again, I was feeling good, as I'd just eaten my usual three bowls of cereal. On Fridays I have my archery lesson. I'm not great, but I'm getting better. Last week I hit the tree just to the right of the target. I'm hoping to nail the actual board soon! (My glasses don't help. Think I'm due for an eye test.)

"About your marriage, Pete," said Mother as she put butter on her toast.

"Yes?" I sat up. "What? What about it?"

"The search for a princess is not going that well," said Mother.

"Oh, what a shame."

"Mmm. I've had quite a few replies, but no one has a daughter of the right age."

"Replies?" I said. "Wait a minute. You mean – your letters actually *arrived*? And you've had *replies*?"

"Well, yes. The post is much, much better since Mr Jones retired."

"Retired?" I cried. "What? When? How come?"

"He gave in his notice a month ago. His granddaughter, Monica, is the kingdom's post girl now. She gallops everywhere on a very fast horse. At last we've got a first-class post service."

"You might as well stop with the marriage plans," I said. "Now there's a princess shortage."

"Don't be silly, darling. This is just the beginning. Next, we advertise. I've already written the advert. Are you listening, Basil? I'm reading out the advert for the *Royal Times*."

"I hope it's short," said my father. "You pay for each word, you know."

My mother produced a card from her pocket.

"*Princess Wanted!*" she read. "*King Basil and Queen Doreen of Skint seek offers for the hand* of their son, Peter, aged 11. Please submit CV and bank statement." She looked up. "What do you think?"

"Not bad," said Father. "I think I could get it shorter."

"No, dear, you couldn't. Are you happy with it, Pete?"

"No," I said. "What's a CV?"

"It's a list of all the interesting things about you. A princess's CV would be all about how beautifully she dances, what charities she supports, the name of her pony, how often she washes her hair, what grade she's reached on recorder. Things like that."

"Who cares?" I cried. "And what sort of nosy parker asks to see someone's bank statement?"

"The sort of nosy parker who wants to know if she'll be bringing a proper dowry, son," said my father. "Like your mother."

"And you, Basil," said Mother. "Don't pretend you're not interested."

"What *is* a dowry?" I asked. All these wedding words were new to me.

"The money the bride gives to the husband," explained Mother.

"You mean I get *paid* to get married?"

"Yes. It's an old-fashioned custom, but we like it, don't we, Basil?"

"I'm not surprised!" I cried. "Talk about one sided. You wouldn't be so keen if I was the princess and you were the ones coughing up."

"You're right there," said my father.

"Well, you're not the princess, you're my handsome prince, and that's all there is to it." Mother stood up. "Have a lovely day, both of you."

She dropped the usual kiss on my father's head, knocked my glasses off as she tried to kiss me and sailed off.

Chapter 2

The Peculiar Pea Thing

A week later, we were at the table again. We usually get together at meal times. It's when Mother asks me about what I do all day, and I tell her I practise hard sums and read clever books. (I don't.)

We were eating late because of bad weather. It was your basic Dark And Stormy Night, and it was black and rainy outside. We needed candles to see by, and Creekie took ages to find them.

It was Friday, so we were eating steamed sprouts and cheese, because Friday night is healthy-eating night in our castle (Mother's idea). Sprouts are not my favourite. They mist up my glasses and taste like wet balls of warmed-up grass. My father and I leave most of them and fill up on the cheese.

For the last few days, nobody had said anything about me getting married. I was hoping Mother and Father had forgotten all about it.

Not so.

"So, darling," said Mother. "You'll want to know about how we got on with your marriage advert. I have to say I'm not very happy."

"You're not?" I said with a thrilled grin.

"No. Only three replies. All from kings of little countries *miles* away. None of them make the Royal Rich List."

"What's the Royal Rich List?"

"The Top Ten Richest Royal families," said my father.

"What number are we?" I enquired.

"Ninety-six. And we'll be even lower if your mother goes and buys the wedding hat she wants. Even though she won't need it for a good few years yet."

"There won't be any money problems once we get the dowry, Basil," said Mother. "A really good dowry will shoot us right up the list. Up there at the top with King Lucky of Plethora."

"Who's he?" I asked. I had never heard of King Lucky of Plethora.

"Number One on the Royal Rich List," Mother told me.

"That's him," agreed my father. "King I-Got-Gold-Mines Lucky of Plethora."

"Dear me. I think Daddy's jealous, Pete," said Mother.

"I am not," said my father.

"You are a bit, dear. But, just think. When a good dowry comes in, we'll be just like him. And then you can stop being so tight, and I shall buy as many hats as I like."

"I don't believe it!" I shouted. "Is money all that matters?"

"Well, no, Pete, of course not. But we must be practical."

"By the way," I said. "Father said something about a thing your family does when they try out princesses. Some peculiar thing with a pea."

"Yes," said my father, a bit annoyed that my mother had said he was jealous and tight. "I left it to you to tell him, Doreen. I can't do it without laughing."

"What made you use the word *peculiar*, Basil?" said my mother.

"Well, it is peculiar," said my father. "You have to admit it's not normal. No one else I know does it."

"That's because it's a family secret," Mother said. She turned to me and looked serious. "Pete. Ignore your father. A very, *very* wise old gypsy woman told this secret to my great-great-great-grandmother when she was a girl. It is a secret as old as the hills."

My father began to laugh but turned it into a yawn.

"So what is it?" I asked. "The pecu— the thing with the pea?"

Mother told me.

I said, "Is this a joke?"

"No."

"You put a pea in the bed and stack loads of blankets and mattresses on top?"

"Yes."

"There's a ladder to get up and down?"

"Yes."

"The princess goes to sleep. And in the morning she's covered in bruises?"

"Yes."

"Not because she fell out of bed. Because of the pea, which she feels digging into her *Princess Skin*."

"Yes."

"And this *Princess Skin* bruises more than ordinary skin, does it?"

"Yes."

"Have *you* got it? *Princess Skin?*"

"Yes, of course."

"So how come you're not covered in bruises?"

"Because I don't keep a pea in the bed. Obviously."

"What about the other girls? The ones who don't bruise?"

"Well, they're fakes."

"That," I said, "is the maddest thing I've ever heard."

"I know," said my father. "It is, you know, Doreen, I keep telling you."

"You may think it's silly," said my mother, "but I think it's important. And you have some strange customs in *your* family too, Basil. Didn't your uncle Dennis walk round the castle dressed as a duck, banging a bucket to make the rain come?"

"But it's not a custom I'm carrying on, is it?" argued my father.

Just then there was a cough from the doorway. Creekie wanted to say something. Just as well someone was around to stop the argument.

"Yes, Creekie?" said Mother.

"You have a visitor, your majesties," said Creekie. "She says she's a princess, but I'm not so sure."

A few girls had turned up at the castle in the last few days. They had read the advert about me having to get married and were pretending to be princesses. So far Creekie hadn't believed any of them and had sent them away.

"Hmm," said Mother. "Who does she say she is?"

"Patsy," someone said. "I'm Princess Patricia of Plethora, but everyone calls me Patsy."

And into the room squished a girl with a small, dripping rucksack on her back. She left a long trail of wet footprints on the floor. She was *soaking*.

We all stared, especially me. I had never met a princess before. I thought they wore pink dresses and glass shoes, not trousers and boots. This one even had a cap on instead of a tiara. I always thought princesses had to have peachy skin and long, glossy hair by law. This one had stumpy plaits and freckles. And I didn't think princesses would squish when they walked.

"Nasty night out," the girl said in a friendly way. "Sorry to drip everywhere. The coach got stuck in the mud, so I got out and walked."

"Apologies, your majesties, I'll bring towels!" said Creekie. He frowned at the girl and snapped, "I don't remember asking you to follow me!"

"Sorry," said Patsy. "I just thought it'd be quicker."

"Look at the mess your boots have made on the floor."

"Sorry. I'll wipe it up."

I was surprised to hear all those "sorry's". *Do princesses say sorry?* I asked myself.

Creekie creaked off to look for towels, and Father, Mother and I were left alone with our new visitor. Mother had gone bright red and looked like she'd stopped breathing. Father was the first one to say anything.

"Well," he said. "This is a surprise. Excuse the mess – just finished eating." He pointed to our dirty green plates on the table. "We weren't expecting you, Patricia."

"Patsy," said Patsy.

"Right. Patsy, Princess of – um – where was it again?"

"Plethora."

Yes, we had heard right. The daughter of the number-one richest king was standing in our dining room!

"Ah," said Father. "I thought that's what you said. King Lucky's daughter. I know of your father. How amazing that he found all those gold mines! And you're his little girl?"

"Not that little," said Patsy. "I'm eleven. Same as Pete." She gave me a grin and added, "Saw your age in the advert."

I felt really embarrassed now. She had seen that awful advert, and she must think I want to get married.

"I'm not here to get married to Pete," she added quickly. "It's just that Dad's having gold flooring put down in the palace, and there's nowhere left for me to play. Someone told me you all live in an old-fashioned castle with turrets and dungeons and a moat and stuff. Can I stay the weekend? I've got my toothbrush."

"Yes!" cried Mother, a bit too loudly. "Yes, dear, stay as long as you like! Very happy to have you! Sit, eat! Have a hot bath! Tell us all about yourself. We have a comfortable spare room. Just need to make up the bed ..."

Mother went rushing out. A bit later, we heard an army of servants thunder up and down the stairs with mattresses and bedding. Patsy looked a bit puzzled. It was clear that something weird was going on, especially as Father and I pretended not to notice.

Creekie came with towels and a mop and creaked off again to organise a bath. We asked Patsy if she wanted some of our leftover sprouts. Wisely, she chose cheese. A maid peeped round the doorway and beckoned to Father. On Friday nights he orders pudding for himself, which he eats in secret in the throne room.

When Father had gone, Patsy and I had a little cheese fight, just to break the ice. We didn't play with the sprouts. Too gross.

We talked about hobbies. I told her about the knightly battles I have in my room and about archery and football. She told me she liked climbing and riding and reading and animals and cooking. She asked if the castle had any ghosts. I said I hadn't seen any, but my glasses aren't that good. I told her that Creekie says he's seen ghost soldiers, but no one else has. Between us, we ate up all the cheese.

Chapter 3

The Tour

The next morning, Father didn't have breakfast with us. That's because on Saturday mornings he meets with angry farmers who are always asking him for more money for the milk they sell us. The meeting has to be early because the farmers have to get back to milk their very expensive cows.

"So," said Mother, looking hard at Patsy's arm. "How did we all sleep?" Patsy had her sleeves rolled up and the only marks I could see were freckles. "Did we all have a comfortable night?"

"It was OK," said Patsy. "It was funny to be that high up. Is that how everyone sleeps around here?"

Patsy had already eaten nearly three bowls of cereal. I'm a good eater too – I picked up my spoon and started to race her.

"Yes," said Mother. "Oh yes, high-up sleeping is quite the thing in Skint."

"I nearly rolled off the bed once. Perhaps I need a safety rope."

"I shall organise it right away," said Mother. "Was the bed soft enough?"

"Plenty. Fifteen mattresses and all those pillows and blankets is soft enough for anybody."

"Mm," said Mother. She sounded puzzled. "So ... you didn't have any bad dreams, I hope?"

"Nope. By the way, this cereal's lovely. We have the expensive stuff at home. This is much nicer."

"I left out some pretty dresses for you," said Mother. "Did you see them?"

"Yes, thanks, but my own clothes are dry now. I don't wear dresses much. They get dirty, and I trip over them."

"Well – fine," said Mother. "I'll – er – I'll just – excuse me, something I must do ..."

And with that, she left the room. At exactly the same time, Patsy and I slammed down our spoons. The cereal race was a draw.

"So," I said. "What do you want to do?"

"Tour of the castle, please."

"OK. Do you want to see the ballroom first?"

"Not especially. I don't do ballroom dancing. I mean, I *dance*, but it's more sort of spinning on my head and jumping around, like this."

Patsy got up, stood on her head, spun a bit and jumped around. There were some fancy leg moves and loads of high-fives. I was impressed and gave her a clap.

"I'll teach you if you like," she said.

"Maybe later. So where shall we go first?"

"Start at the top, work our way down."

*

The wind nearly blew us away when we stepped out onto the battlements. It was freezing, so we didn't stay out long. Just long enough to throw down a couple of stones and watch them splash in the moat below.

"We could climb around out here," said
Patsy. "Hang from the high bits and creep along
the ledges. When it's not so windy. Maybe
tomorrow?"

"Hm," I said. "Maybe." I'm a bit nervous about climbing high.

Next, we went to the armoury. Patsy wanted to see all the bloodthirsty stuff – the swords and lances and battle axes. It's really dirty up there – full of rusty metal and cobwebs. There's loads of other junk in the armoury. Legless tables, old suitcases, grubby paintings. Cracked mirror. The cat basket.

We tried on some armour. It was fun. There was loads to choose from. Helmets, curly metal shoes, breastplates, chain mail. Giggling like idiots, we tried on all sorts. We clonked around and waved our swords. We saluted each other. We waggled the visors up and down. We did silly poses in front of the mirror.

Patsy said, "I'd come and dress up in armour every day if I lived here."

I said, "It's not that much fun on your own. After a bit, the old metal smell gets to you."

Patsy said, "That's true. But we'll come again tomorrow, won't we?"

After the armoury, we went down a floor and inspected each other's rooms. She really liked my model knight collection. And she admired the drawing I did of Darby, the postman's donkey, last year. He's good to draw because he moves so much slower than your pencil.

"He's lovely," said Patsy. "I like donkeys. Can I meet him?"

"Tomorrow," I said. "If you're still here."

"Oh, I'll be here. I'm having fun. I see your bed's a normal height. I thought your mum said everyone around here sleeps high up."

"Not everyone," I admitted. "She's fibbing a bit there."

"I thought so. Come and see what she's done in my room."

I went and I saw.

It was ridiculous. The stack of mattresses and bedding was so high there was hardly room to squeeze on top. A tall ladder was over on one side.

"Well, look at that!" said Patsy. "I think the bed's got even higher! My nose'll touch the ceiling tonight!"

"It's just some peculiar old custom they have in my mother's family," I said. "I'd tell you, but it's a secret."

"Great!" said Patsy. "I love weird old secret customs. We don't have them in our family. Dad's a new sort of king. He likes modern palaces and golden coaches and expensive restaurants. Where next?"

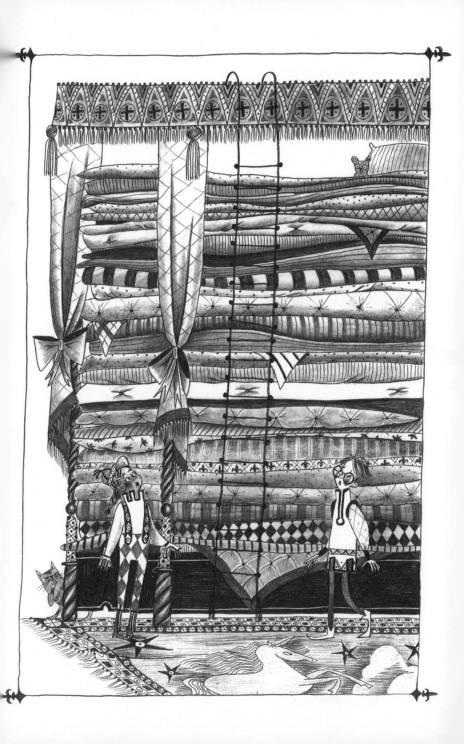

Next, we poked our heads into the throne room. There are three thrones. One for Father, one for Mother and one for me.

"Like the three bears," whispered Patsy. "Father Bear's fast asleep, look."

My father was slumped on his throne with his mouth open. The milk farmers must have worn him out. Watching him snore was no fun, so we tiptoed away.

We went into the library next. You can take out three books at a time. Patsy took ages to choose. In the end she got one about pirates, a cookery book with a picture of a chocolate cake on the cover and one about boxing.

"Boxing?" I said.

"Yep. Dad gave me the money for dancing lessons, but I'm going to spend it on boxing."

"Good for you," I said. Well, she could dance already – I knew that.

"Is there a secret passage in this library?" asked Patsy.

"Yep," I said. "It leads down to the dungeons. Watch."

I pulled out the third book from the left on the biggest bookcase and the bookcase swung open to show a dark doorway with stone steps leading down.

"Wow!" said Patsy. "Spooky! Let's go down!"

"Not now," I said. "It's lunch-time."

"Later, right?" said Patsy, and I agreed.

Next, we went across to the kitchens. It's nice in the kitchens. Always warm and busy and smelling good. Cook was making biscuits and let us stir. Patsy showed her the library cookbook and they decided to make the chocolate cake as well, which was fine by me.

"Yer ma was here earlier," Cook said to me as I broke eggs into a bowl. "Her Majesty, bless her." Cook is a fan of Mother.

"Oh?" I said. "What did she want?"

"A sprout," said Cook. "A big, raw, hard sprout. It's all this healthy-eating thing she's into."

"I don't think she wants to eat it," I said, remembering the mattress tower in Patsy's room. "I think she just wants to ... put it somewhere."

"Where?" asked Cook.

"It's a secret," I said. "Shall I put in the sugar now?"

*

The biscuits turned out great, and the cake was fantastic. We ate almost all of it but left a small slice for my father, who loves cake. Then we went and skimmed stones in the moat. Mine went furthest, but Patsy's stones bounced more times. Then she showed me a couple of dance moves. I tried spinning on my head, but my glasses fell off. Like my archery, it needs more practice.

We had a walk around the grounds because my head hurt and we both felt a bit sick after all that cake. I didn't go near the archery targets because I had a feeling Patsy would be better than me. But she saw them. "Let's do that!" she shouted.

I said, "Not now. I'm still a bit dizzy."

"OK," said Patsy. "Tomorrow."

When my head felt better, we climbed a tree. I don't mind climbing if it's not too high. Both of us agreed it was a perfect tree for a tree house. We found some spare planks behind the gardener's hut and dragged them back to the tree so we could make a tree house the next day. By then it was tea time, so we went back and finished off my father's slice of cake. We just kept cutting bits off, and it got smaller and smaller until it was gone.

It was too late to visit the dungeons. Creekie locks them at night. Instead, we went and played a long, complicated battle with my knights. Patsy added a few new rules of her own, so it took a long time.

"We'll finish it tomorrow," said Patsy, yawning. "Night, Pete."

We didn't bother with supper. All that cake. Yuck.

Chapter 4

A Lot to Pack In

The next day, there was so much to pack in we made a list. It went:

Climb the battlements (maybe)
Dress up in armour (again)
Meet donkey
Practise dance moves
Do archery (maybe)
Finish knightly battle
Build tree house
Visit dungeons

All that on top of just walking around. It seemed a lot. But it was fun to make plans with someone else. Patsy wasn't turning out to be anything like I was expecting.

With all these things to do, we didn't plan to hang around once we'd finished breakfast, but Mother wanted to talk to us.

"And where are you two off to in such a hurry?"

"The battlements," I said. "Maybe. But it might be too cold."

"First things first, darling. I like a little chat with my boy and his little friend first thing in the morning, and so does Daddy, don't you, Basil?"

"Mm," muttered my father, who didn't.

"How was your night, Patsy, dear?" asked Mother.

"Fine. It's better with the safety rope."

"Nothing that went bump in the night?"

"By that she means did anything give you a *real* bump," said my father. "She's not asking if you saw a ghost."

He avoided Mother's glare.

"No," said Patsy. "But I wish there *was* a ghost. I'd love that."

"Well, there isn't, I'm afraid," said Mother. "Creekie keeps saying he's seen ghost soldiers, but no one believes him. Is that a little bruise I see on your hand, Patsy dear?"

"No, it's ink. I wrote the knightly battle scores on it."

"Oh, hmm. Well." My mother frowned, shook her head, got up and rushed out of the room muttering to herself.

She was beginning to panic, I could tell.
The pea thing wasn't working! For two nights
running, Patsy's Princess Skin had no bruises or
marks at all! What was happening? I knew my
mother was going to ring up my aunties to ask
what to do now. Must it be a *round* vegetable
in the bed? Or even green? Should she try
something sharper, like a carrot? Or could it
be – Oh no! Oh surely not! – could it simply be
that *the girl who said she was Princess Patricia
of Plethora, daughter of super-rich King Lucky,
was a fake*???

*

Patsy and I had a great day. We didn't fit in
everything we'd planned, of course. We skipped
the battlements, thank goodness. We spent
another hour dressing up in armour. Then we
tried to choose between the other stuff:

Visit donkey
Practise dancing

Archery
Knightly battle
Tree house
Dungeon

It was a toss-up between the donkey, the tree house and the dungeon. The donkey won.

*

Mr Jones the postman lives in a cottage in the wood with his granddaughter, Monica. It's a comfy little house with roses around the door. There are flowers and an apple tree and a bird table. Because he is – well, was – a postman, he has a red post box at the bottom of his garden as a decoration.

Darby the donkey lives around the back, in a paddock. It's a nice paddock with leafy trees and plenty of thistles to nibble.

"I hear you're retired, Mr Jones," I said as I walked up the path. He was sitting on the garden bench doing nothing.

"That's right, Pete, I am."

"This is my friend Patsy."

"Pleased to meet you, ducks."

"Hello, Mr Jones," said Patsy. "I like your post box. Are you happy being retired?"

"Not really." He gave a sigh. "I thought it would be lovely, but the time drags something shocking."

"Does Darby like it?" I asked.

"Nope. Gone right off his food. Feels a bit left out of things, I reckon. Sees Monica go galloping off leaving him with nothing to do and nowhere to go. Monica's taken over the round, see."

"So I heard," I said. "Poor old Darby."

"Go round the back, give him a whistle," said Mr Jones. "See if he wants an apple. I gave him a few leftover postcards, his favourite treat, but he turned his nose up."

We went round the back with some apples, but Darby didn't seem too happy to see us or our foody gifts. He didn't bother to turn round to see who we were. His ears were droopy and he didn't even look up.

"He's not himself," I said. "He's usually friendly."

"Bored," said Patsy. "Depressed. Needs to get out."

"You could be right," said Mr Jones, from behind us. "Missing the exercise."

"I bet he'd like someone to ride him round a bit," said Patsy. "Give him a purpose in life. Can I?"

"Be my guest," said Mr Jones.

So Patsy went over, covered Darby's nose with kisses and climbed on. Darby didn't mind. She rode him all around the paddock. Then I had a go. Not the nose kissing, just the riding. He wasn't as slow as usual. In fact, he seemed really frisky.

Some little kids from the local village came by, and they all had rides too. When they finished, they kissed and patted him and fed him thistles.

"Looks like you've both got a new job," said Patsy to Mr Jones. "Giving little kids donkey rides. When summer comes, you can do it at the seaside."

"Good suggestion," said Mr Jones. "We might just do that."

We came away feeling pleased with ourselves. That was our good deed for the day.

*

It was time to build the tree house. It's hard to lay planks across branches. I fell off and cracked my glasses. At least I had an excuse not to do archery now.

When we got the planks in position, we got a tablecloth from Cook and some black paint from the gardener and made a pirate flag. Then Patsy went and got her library book and read out bloodthirsty pirate facts, and we sat in the tree as if we were in a boat on the high seas.

We went to the kitchen for a sandwich. Cook told us that Mother had been in and gone off with a turnip, a cabbage and a handful of carrots. She said that Mother was in a funny mood. I said nothing.

We still hadn't fitted in my dance practice, so we did that in the corridor. Patsy said I was almost getting the hang of it. By then, it was getting a bit dark. But we still had two things to do. Finish the knightly battle and visit the dungeons.

"Dungeons first!" said Patsy. "We'll take the secret passage from the library!"

"It'll be dark," I said. "There will be cobwebs."

"We'll put on armour," said Patsy. "To protect us from ghosts and spiders."

We found some candles and crept up to the armoury, where we put on our favourite bits of armour. Then we clanked down to the library.

"Can I open the secret door this time?" asked Patsy.

"Go ahead," I said. I've done it loads of times, so it's no big deal.

Patsy pulled the book out and the shelves swung open. We stepped in and started off down the stone steps.

There are 90 steps. They go on and on. At last we got to the bottom. The dungeons stretched out ahead, dark and full of cobwebs.

"What's down here anyway?" asked Patsy.

"Sacks of potatoes. Jars of jam. Creekie stores food down here."

"No chains? Bones? Ghosts? Rats? No real dungeon stuff?"

"No. Sorry."

"Do we have to tramp all the way back up those steps again?"

"No, there's another door into the courtyard, next to the kitchens."

"Then let's go. I've had enough of this armour – I'm all sweaty. And we can finish off the knightly battle, like we said we would."

And that's what we did.

*

Later, I was lying in bed thinking about what a good day it had been. Patsy wasn't at all what I'd been expecting a princess to be like. She was – well, normal. Friendly. Fun.

But as I lay there thinking about my new friend, there was a tap on the door, and Mother loomed in the doorway. "She's a fake," Mother declared.

"What?" I asked.

"Your little friend Patsy. She's no princess. I'm almost sure of it. I suspected it from the beginning, of course. You only had to look at the clothes. Unless she's covered with bruises in the morning, she's going. Straight after breakfast."

And with that, Mother stomped off.

Chapter 5

Goodbye

The following morning, everyone was very quiet at the breakfast table. Father read the paper as Patsy and I stormed through our usual three bowls of cereal. Mother sat frowning with her arms folded, waiting to pounce.

"Well," she said as we laid down our spoons. "I hope you're all packed and ready to go, Miss Whoever-you-are. Back to Wherever-you-came-from. Because you can't stay here a minute longer."

"I know," said Patsy. "I have to go home to Plethora. But I've had a lovely time. Thanks for having me."

"Don't lie!" snapped Mother. "Don't pretend to be King Lucky's daughter, you naughty girl. Because I know you're not!"

"I think I'll take this to the throne room," said my father, standing up with his paper.

"Sit down, Basil. I'm not doing this on my own. You need to tell this cheeky girl that I've seen through her barefaced lies. Pete needs a real princess to marry, and she's not one! My test does not lie!"

"Steady on, Doreen," said my father.

"I am going upstairs to lie down," said Mother. "And when I come downstairs, I want her gone!"

And with that, she swept out.

"Sorry about that," my father and I mumbled.

"That's all right," said Patsy. "I've got to go anyway. I need to get home in time for my first boxing lesson. Oh ..." She reached under the table and took out a bag. She handed it to my father, saying, "Give these to Her Majesty when she's feeling better, please. It's just some random vegetables she put in the bed. I kept finding them before I got in. A turnip, a sprout, a cabbage, some carrots, a pea ..."

"Ah," I said. "Yes. Well, that's to do with—"

"The weird old family custom. I guessed that. Anyway, there's enough there to make a nice soup."

*

"It's a shame you have to go," I said. It was later that morning, and I was seeing Patsy off.

"But I'll come again," said Patsy. "If your mum will have me!"

She was leaning out of the coach window. It was a very flashy golden coach. The coachman had been staying at the village inn. He said he'd paid out a fortune to the local teenagers to keep an eye on it. It hadn't stopped them painting two yellow stripes on the horse.

"Next weekend?" I said.

"You bet. We can take a raft out on the moat and play five-a-side football. The kitchen maids want to get up a team – I asked them. And I want to try archery, so get your glasses fixed."

"OK," I said. "It was fun last night, wasn't it?"

We looked at each other and giggled. Creekie was really happy – he'd spotted two ghost soldiers coming out of the dungeons and creeping into the courtyard. Now he was

going around telling everyone that the castle is definitely haunted, just like he'd always said. I think we made his day.

"Don't forget to practise your dance moves," said Patsy.

"OK. Good luck with the boxing."

"Thanks. Bye, Pete."

"Bye, Patsy. See you soon."

We both waved until she was out of sight. Mother came running up just as the coach turned the corner. My father came sauntering along behind, in no hurry.

"Bother!" said Mother. "Just too late."

"Did you have something to say to her, by any chance?" I asked.

"Well, yes. Your father handed me the vegetables and explained that she threw them out of the bed *before* she got in. That's why she had no bruises. So despite the trousers and that awful cap, she must be a proper princess after all. I would have known if I'd seen the golden coach."

"So you were going to say sorry," I said.

"Well … yes. But you and Daddy should also say sorry to me for sneering at an old family custom. You see, Basil? That wise old gypsy woman was right after all!"

"If it makes you happy, dear," said my father.

"So can Patsy sleep in a normal bed next time she comes to stay?" I asked.

"Definitely," said Mother.

"No more peas?

"No more peas."

And you won't embarrass us by talking about weddings and stuff?"

"W-e-e-ll …"

"And you can promise to stop kissing me at breakfast."

"All right, darling," said Mother. "I promise." And she scooped me up and dropped a huge smacker on my cheek.

Our books are tested
for children and young people by
children and young people.

Thanks to everyone who consulted on
a manuscript for their time and effort in
helping us to make our books better
for our readers.